Gilbert and Sullivan's Improba Musical: The Fringe Lozei

Script and Lyrics

Susan Ellerby

Inspired by the operettas of W.S. Gilbert and Arthur Sullivan, with new lyrics set to Sullivan's music

First performed by Coily Dart Theatre at the Edinburgh Festival Fringe in 2017

Reviews from Edinburgh Festival Fringe 2017

"*Wryly amusing … A labyrinthine plot in the finest G&S tradition*" (Fringe Review).

"*An easy show to recommend to lovers of Gilbert and Sullivan… It is all very good fun; witty and self-referential in exactly the right way…The point of the show is essentially to amuse the audience with a loving parody of G&S operettas and make fun of the Fringe while doing so. In this, it succeeds admirably*" (Broadway Baby).

"*Clearly this production has been devised by Gilbert & Sullivan aficionados, and is a labour of love … It is pleasing that the temptation to cherry-pick from only the most popular Savoy Opera musical numbers is resisted*" (Broadway World).

"*New lyrics of considerable invention … An inventive and enjoyable romp… Were Arthur Sullivan to emerge in ghostly presence at a future performance, like one of the portraits in Ruddigore, perhaps he would think again about that dreaded lozenge plot of Gilbert's …*" (Sardines Magazine).

"A delightful collection of Gilbertian ideas and plot points, married to Sullivan's music … An absolutely delectable slice of a Gilbert and Sullivan sponge cake, liberally covered in jam and cream" (MusicalTalk Podcast).

Acknowledgments

I hope you enjoy reading this script as much as I have enjoyed writing it. The original idea would not have progressed to this stage without the tremendous encouragement and support I have received from others along the way, for which I feel very fortunate.

Firstly my thanks to Steve Bruce, Dettie Ellerby, Paul Smart and Joe Allen – with whom I tentatively shared an early version of the show. They took time to give detailed feedback, and have since provided ongoing encouragement and helpful advice throughout the whole creative process, for which I am immensely grateful.

Heartfelt thanks also to the original Coily Dart Theatre cast and crew who brought the show to life at the Edinburgh Festival Fringe in August 2017: Sofia Aguiar, Elizabeth Fenner, Eilidh Gibson, Daniel Grooms, Chris Higgins, Norman Hockley, Becky Norton, Ben Heslop, Patsy Hockley and Mike Ellerby. They were an inspiration to work with and, without their talent, dedication and skill, the show would not have evolved into this publication.

Finally, the most significant acknowledgement must be to the genius of W.S. Gilbert and Arthur Sullivan. The idea for this show was inspired by their operettas and all the music used is from existing Sullivan compositions.

Susan Ellerby

Writer and Director
Coily Dart Theatre
coilydart@gmail.com
@coilydart

Contents

Introduction

This show was originally written for Coily Dart Theatre's production at The Edinburgh Festival Fringe in 2017, where it achieved a sell-out run and was awarded a Fringe Laurel.

Set at the Fringe, the show follows the quest of two companies, each going to extreme lengths to secure a good review. The plot includes the usual Gilbertian elements: an abandoned baby, sense of duty, love across ranks and an implausible, contrived finale. The picture is completed by unusual flat-sharing arrangements and a magic lozenge. The songs feature all-new lyrics set to Sullivan's music, with melodies drawn from every operetta.

The aim of the original production was to entertain Fringe audiences and showcase new talent, while also introducing more people to Gilbert and Sullivan and stimulating further creativity and innovation in the Gilbert and Sullivan mould.

The show was initially intended as a Fringe "one-off", but the reception received exceeded all expectations. Following the tremendous audience response, and encouraging reviews, it seemed appropriate to publish the script and lyrics in case others may enjoy reading, or even performing, the show.

The music that accompanies the lyrics is referenced by the name of the operetta and the name of the melody used. Some of the musical numbers have been shortened, by reducing the number of verses to which lyrics have been set. Where this happens it is indicated in the script. Other than this, Sullivan's music and harmonies have not been altered. The melodies for each of the musical interludes are also referenced.

Optional notes around props, some of the staging, and the co-ordination of scene changes have been included in this text, reflecting the setting of the original performance. To put the notes into context, it may be helpful to know a little about the original approach used.

The show has the flexibility to be performed with either a small or large cast. The original production featured a cast of six (four of whom played multiple roles). The choreography and movement in the original production mirrored the style frequently seen in Gilbert and Sullivan performances.

When performed at the Fringe the show was a fast paced production, with rapid scene and costume changes, creating a running time of 50 minutes. When a scene ended, the cast turned to look upstage and froze in position for 4 seconds. The lighting then changed and a brief musical interlude began. At this point the cast changed the props/costumes as required, then moved into their positions for the next scene, standing with their backs to the audience for 4 seconds as the musical interlude completed. When the musical interlude ended the lighting resumed and they turned around in character to begin the next scene.

In the original production the Gilbert and Sullivan characters blended into the background between their acting interjections. The piano was on stage (upstage left) and they sat behind the piano (between their acting sections), singing along with all of the choruses and four part harmonies.

Costumes and props used in the original production

In the original setting the props were held in four boxes on stage and in one box backstage. The distribution of costumes and props between the boxes is noted in Appendix A.

Costumes

Gilbert and Sullivan: Dark 3-piece lounge suit and ties (Gilbert's tie "jazzy" and Sullivan's plain)
Other Male characters: Blue denim jeans, white T-shirts and black canvas shoes
Female characters: Blue denim shorts, black opaque tights, white T-shirts and black canvas shoes
Fred and crew: Red zip up hoodies (Fred's has a copy of a Winnie the Pooh book in the pocket attached to the hoodie by a string and safety pin)
Phoebe and crew: Blue lanyards with name on the identity tag in large print
Ralph: Dark waistcoat with name badge pinned on and an A4 size Maths book
Gus and Mark: Dark 'beanie' type hats
Buffet car attendant: Checked hat
Flight attendant: Oval flight attendant hat
SoCoCoCo: Arty scarf and sunglasses
John: Black cape, magic wand, a few playing cards, and a tin of "magic lozenges" (wrapped boiled sweets)

Props

Large vintage style case/trunk (long enough to act as a bar/counter when upended)
Copy of a vocal score from every operetta – old style if possible
2 empty soft drink cans
4 stools
3 mobile phones
Something that looks like an ipad/tablet
Various flyers (including two groups of similar ones)
2 Fringe programmes
2 copies of Three Weeks newspaper
4 copies of The Scotsman newspaper
Scottish £5 note
2 light up plastic glasses

14

Songs: melody titles and source

1: Then one of us will be a Queen: The Gondoliers

2: Hark the Hour of Ten: Trial by Jury

3: Here upon we're both agreed: The Yeomen of The Guard

4: Ring Forth ye Bells: The Sorcerer

5: If you want a receipt for that popular mystery: Patience

6: If you give me your attention: Princess Ida

7: None Shall Part us from each other: Iolanthe

8: Brightly dawns our wedding day: The Mikado

9: I've Jibe and joke: The Yeomen of The Guard

10: Kind Captain I've important information: H.M.S. Pinafore

11: When the night wind howls: Ruddigore

12: Bridegroom and bride: The Gondoliers

13: Spurn not the nobly born: Iolanthe

14: But tell me, who's the youth: H.M.S. Pinafore

14a: The nightingale sighed: H.M.S. Pinafore

14b: A maiden fair to see   : H.M.S. Pinafore

15: Hail Poetry: The Pirates of Penzance

16: After much debate internal: Patience

The Show

As audience enter

Large vintage trunk open centre stage, with old scores draped over the sides (one from every show).
Gilbert and Sullivan are sitting upstage left with the Piano in front of them (at 90 degrees).
The other four cast members are sitting on stools at back of stage (a black box adjacent to each with props in – distribution listed in Appendix A). Each of the four are leafing through an old score.

Song 1 Melody: Then one of us will be a Queen (The Gondoliers)

All:
Verse 1 sing as "La's", chorus as "La's"
Verse 2 sing as "Ba's", chorus as "La's"
Verse 3 sing as "Da's", chorus as "La's"
Verse 4 sing as "Pa's", chorus as "La's".

If longer is needed to seat an audience, then repeat Verse 3 and chorus (as many times as needed) before proceeding to Verse 4.

As piano is finishing, Gilbert and Sullivan walk to the front of the stage. When Gilbert and Sullivan begin their dialogue the cast are still.

Sullivan: My dear Gilbert I have told you before, the answer is No! No, No, categorically No. We are not writing an operetta about a magic lozenge.
Gilbert: Please Arthur – I've made some tweaks, just hear me out … Last night I had a dream that we were transported 100 years into the future, to Edinburgh! The city was hosting the largest arts festival in the world – over 50,000 performances, all within three weeks.
Sullivan: That's it, Gilbert, yet another of your ludicrous ideas!
Gilbert: Look, you have an hour to spare – sit over here and see what you think. I've got some scores and we can join in! I've re-hashed your old tunes to some new lyrics.
Sullivan: Nothing new there then.

Scene 1: Setting the scene for the show

Gilbert and Sullivan return to their seats behind the piano as "Hark the Hour of Ten" begins. During the piano introduction the other four cast members take out the scores from the trunk and place them by the piano, moving the trunk out of the way to downstage right before starting to sing the opening song.

Song 2 Melody: Hark the Hour of Ten (Trial by Jury)

All:
Welcome to our latest Fringe show
G and S themed, as you may know.
Liberties with the Libretto
Score's not been impinged.

Sullivan wrote music glorious,
Gilbert's plots are meritorious
For this Topsy Turvy show
Located at the fringe.

Welcome to our latest Fringe show
G and S themed, as you may know.
Liberties with the Libretto
Score's not been impinged.

Liberties with the Libretto
Score's not been impinged.

There are only four of us here,
Changing parts we'll try and make clear,
Bigger cast would have been too dear,
Budget plan unhinge.

Sullivan wrote music glorious,
Gilbert's plots are meritorious
For this Topsy Turvy show
Located at the Fringe.

So sit back, enjoy the journey
Recognise some themes you may know.
Copyright, says our attorney,
Has not been infringed.

Scene change: Short piano extract from: Little Maid of Arcadee - Thespis

During the musical interlude Mabel and Ida move the trunk to downstage right (upended/half open) to act as a pub/bar then exit and put on their hoodies offstage. Gus and Mark put on beanie hats, each pick up a can, then bring 2 stools to the front of the bar, sit down and place cans on the bar.

Scene 2: *Gus and Mark planning the flat rental*

SETTING: A PUB, FAR FROM EDINBURGH

Gus and Mark sitting at a bar.

Gus: So Mark - Still nobody wanting our help this year?
Mark: No – can't believe it. Our 10th Fringe too!
Gus: Still going though?
Mark: Daft question Gus. Of course! Staying with the usual crowd if you need a floor to sleep on.
Gus: Thanks - it really is so expensive getting somewhere central to rent.
Mark: It'll be so strange not helping with a show this time. I so love doing the change overs.
Gus: I love the challenge of trying to get the set in and out in record time.
Mark: 4 minutes is your personal best isn't it Gus?
Gus: That's right – and it involved shifting three settees … and an aga.
Mark: Well, it'll be strange just being punters, that's for sure.
Gus: Yes – money's going to be tight too if we're not working.
(Pause)
Mark: By the way Gus, I was sorry to hear your Gran had passed away. I used to love visiting her when we were up in Edinburgh.
Gus: Thanks. Mum wants me to clear her sheltered flat out while we're up at the Fringe before she sells it. I must remember that the warden always imposes those weird access restrictions for non-residents while the Festival's on.
Gus and Mark: (*both put on affected voices*): "How many times must we tell you boys that, during the Fringe, access is only permitted between the hours of 7 and 8 in the morning and 7 and 8 in the evening" *(both laugh).*
Mark: Her flat was so handy to pop into for a coffee and a chat.
Gus: Yes, such a lovely flat, and so CENTRAL *(look as if the penny drops).*
Mark: (*excitedly*): Hey, Gus - Are you thinking what I'm thinking? We could rent it out to someone - easily – that would increase our fringe budget!
Gus: We **could** rent it out to some ONE… but, thanks to those strange access restrictions - double your expectations my friend!
(Mark looks puzzled)
Gus: "List and learn" *(affected voice)*: … "List and learn!"

Song 3 Melody: Here upon we're both agreed (The Yeomen of The Guard)
(Omit second verse melody)

Gus: We will advertise the flat

As two rentals,
Fundamentals.
Mark: One for night and one for day,
A no brainer
What's not plainer.

Gus: Set A enter 8pm,
Post cavorting
Fringe supporting.

Mark: Set B's left there just before,
At half seven
Repossession!

Gus: At half seven.
Mark: Repossession!
Gus: At half seven.
Mark: Repossession!

Gus and Mark together (these lines at the same time):
Gus: At half seven, repossession, at half seven.
Mark: Repossession, at half seven, repossession.

Gus and Mark together (harmony)
12 hours later, same again
Half hour switch we must attain
Move A out
Move B in
Move B out
A in again
Half hour switch we must attain!

(Omit second verse melody and go straight to end section)

Gus: We will up our rent.
Mark: To a great extent!
Gus: We will up our rent.
Mark: To a great extent!
Gus and Mark: We will up our rent, up our rent, up our rent, up our rent
We will up it, up it to a great extent!

Scene change: Short piano extract from: I have a song to sing, O! – The Yeomen of The Guard

Mabel and Ida put hoodies on backstage, then enter and move trunk out of the way, upended, downstage left and put stools and cans back. Mark (Fred) and Gus (Rupert) change into hoodies then Fred puts a Fringe programme onto furthest stage right stool.

Scene 3: Fred's team preparing to go to the Fringe

SETTING: A REHEARSAL ROOM

During the introduction to the next song Mabel, Rupert and Ida act out finishing their last rehearsal – bows etc. Fred is directing.

Song 4 Melody: Ring Forth ye Bells (The Sorcerer)

All:
That's it, we're done
Our last run through -
So hope we've won
A good review.
Create a storm
Then go on tour,
We're so on form
Five stars, for sure.

Women:
We have got quite a late slot -
Men:
It's 10.30 in the evening -
Women:
But the cost was reduced -
Men:
For our budget that was great,

Women:
And our flat has weird access -
Men:
By half seven finish sleeping -
Women:
In the evening then back –

Men:
In the morning time at eight!

All:
And our flat has weird access -
By half seven finish sleeping -
In the evening then back -
In the morning time at eight!

Women:
It suits us fine,
We'll be all right -

All:
We'll do our show,
Stay out 'til dawn.
We'll do our show,
Stay out 'til dawn.

All:
That's it, we're done
Our last run through -
So hope we've won
A good review.
Create a storm
Then go on tour,
We're so on form
Five stars, for sure.

Create a storm
Then go on tour,
We're so on form
Five stars, for sure.

That's it, we're done
Our last run through
So hope we've won
A good review.

Now we're done,
Let's get gone,

Echo from Sullivan: "Angelina" *(sing as in Trial by Jury)*.

Angelina enters to Chorus of Bridesmaids music (Trial by Jury) - music continues as she rushes down the aisle and pushes past Ralph to get into her seat. Lanyard is swung over her right shoulder.

Angelina: Thank you very much.
Ralph: It's OK – *(takes lanyard/name tag, looks at it then puts in correct position)*: – Angelina.
(Eyes meet, both smile soppy smiles: Triangle "ding" and lighting effect)
Angelina: Ooh – you're a Director, how exciting *(brushes hair back with right hand - Ralph catches sight of her elbow)*.
Ralph: Yes, I'm taking a show up to the Fringe. What an elbow!
Angelina: I'm sorry *(looking perplexed)*?
Ralph: My show is a Shakespeare inspired devised piece that is a mixture of physical theatre, burlesque, mime and circus – performed in an immersive space with acapella musical interludes and elements of comedic improvisation. It's called "The Semitoned Pirates". I have to say, I had a very difficult job knowing which section of the programme to put it in. How about you?
Angelina: Oh, I am just going to work at one of the venues. You, a Director though – you must be so excited!
Ralph: Not really…you see… I am not very keen on theatre.
Angelina: Well, why are you here then?
Ralph: You may not understand, but I am the son of ...
Air hostess interruption: Please ensure all seat belts are fastened for take off.
Ralph: *(irritated at the interruption says more loudly)*: I am the son of …
Air hostess: Please ensure all hand luggage is placed under the seat in front of you.
Ralph: *(more irritated and more loudly)*: The only son of …
Air hostess: Cabin crew prepare for take off.
Ralph:*(loudly then looks embarrassed)*: SoCoCoCo!
Air hostess: *(walks down to take seat behind Ralph)*: "Shhh" *(sits and picks up the other Fringe programme)*.
Angelina: Well I don't see what difference that makes *(looks at name badge on his waistcoat)* - Ralph.

Song 6 Melody: If you give me your attention (Princess Ida)
(Omit second verse melody)

Ralph:
It's Raiph, the L is silent
And yes, Schwenck's my middle name.
My parents are both "in the biz"

And therein lies the blame.

They forced me into theatre.
Oh that I could study maths,
But on drama they insisted
And they chose my career path.

Their great SoCoCoCo theatre troupe
Is doing rather well.
They need a new producer
And I'm lined up for that hell.

To real theatre lovers its Utopian, I'm sure.
For mathematic buffs like me
I find it's such a bore

But my duty's clear!

(Omit second verse melody)

Angelina:
Well, why don't you just tell them?
I'm sure they would understand.
You're such a lovely person
Maybe I could lend a hand.

I'm going to the fringe to work
At venue seventy.
I'm here and I'll support you,
Even let you in for free.

Ralph:
I'm sorry you don't follow
I couldn't possibly.
Though your right elbow's perfect
It's your ranking, don't you see?

As son of SoCoCoCo
Our Fringe status gap is wide.
To date a venue worker
It would hurt my parents' pride,

So my duty's clear!

Angelina: His duty's clear!

All: My/His duty's clear!

Scene change: Short piano extract from: Now to the banquet we press – The Sorcerer

Ralph takes stool and maths book to back of stage, takes waistcoat off and puts buffet attendant's hat on. Angelina takes stool to back of stage, takes lanyard off, helps Phoebe put trunk in place (upended to form train buffet counter) then stands downstage right as the train announcer. Air Hostess (Phoebe) puts stool to back of stage, takes hat off and puts lanyard on then helps Angelina with the trunk. Passenger (Fred) takes the stool and fringe programmes to the back of stage and puts hoodie on.

Scene 6: Fred and Phoebe meeting on the train

SETTING: TRAIN BUFFET CARRIAGE

Phoebe and Fred are walking towards the central buffet counter (upended trunk) from opposite sides of the stage. The attendant is behind the counter looking fed up. All are shaking as if on a train. All lurch on word "centre" from train announcer (see below) and at this point Phoebe spots Fred's book as it falls.

Train Announcer: This train is for Edinburgh Waverley Station. Next stop Newcastle. The buffet is now open and is towards the centre of the train. *(announcer exits)*

Phoebe: After you.
Fred: No, after you.
Phoebe: It's fine.
Fred: No, it's fine.
(Both laugh, eyes meet, both smile soppy smiles: Triangle "ding" and Lighting effect)

Attendant: Can you hurry up please.
Phoebe: What sandwiches do you have? Egg? Ham?
Attendant: Strawberry Jam. That's all that's left I'm afraid, though we do have some fancy sounding buns that aren't selling.
Phoebe: Oh it's OK, I'll just have a sausage roll.
Fred: Same for me please.

(Both laugh)
Attendant: *(taps nose knowingly; others look puzzled)*: Sorry none of those either.
Phoebe: We do seem to have similar tastes – I can see you're reading A.A.Milne. My favourite author.
Fred: *(gets the book out of his pocket, attached to his hoodie by a string)*: There's a bit of a tale behind this – you see I was abandoned as a baby on the steps of the Savoy Theatre *(both freeze in a pose looking to the distance. Piano plays: "The Nightingale sighed for the moon's bright ray" melody/lighting effect).* Tucked under the blankets was this first edition. I keep it with me always.
Attendant: *(rolls eyes)*: Move along now please.
(Phoebe and Fred move away from the buffet)
Fred: Fortunately, a member of the pit orchestra found me and brought me up as his own.
Attendant: *(jokingly)*: The violins *(mimes playing violins).*
Fred: *(seriously)*: No, second trombone actually.
(attendant exits centre back)
Phoebe: What an unusual story. Have you heard that they have opened an A.A. Milne themed pub in Edinburgh this year?
Fred: Wow really – well, look, would you like to meet up there? Maybe after my first reviews are in. I'm hoping to have something to celebrate.
Phoebe: I'd love to. I could stay with my friend Elsie that night. Our flat has some funny access restrictions ... don't ask!
Fred: Great. What's this A.A.Milne themed pub called?
Phoebe: Oh - The Pooh Bar.

Song 7 Melody: None Shall Part us from each other (Iolanthe)
(Omit second verse melody)

Fred: I shall see you, at the Pooh Bar
When the first reviews are in.
Phoebe: We seem so ideally suited
Our romance can now begin.

Fred and Phoebe: We seem so ideally suited
Our romance can now begin.

Fred and Phoebe (harmony):
We both share a love of theatre
A.A.Milne, and his Pooh Bear
We'll enjoy our first drink later
A predictable affair.

We both share a love of theatre,
AA Milne, and his Pooh Bear.
We'll enjoy our first drink later,
A predictable affair.

Scene change: Short piano extract from: Welcome to our hearts again, Iolanthe!
- Iolanthe

Fred and Phoebe move the trunk out of the way, to stage right.
Fred picks up batch of similar flyers.
Phoebe picks up an iPad and phone.

Scene 7: Phoebe completing her first reviews

SETTING: OUTSIDE THE THEATRES AT RALPH AND FRED'S FRINGE
VENUE

Fred alone upstage centre with a handful of flyers calling in the show.

Fred: Idle Auntie, Idle Auntie *(words lilting to the Iolanthe appropriate tune).*

Phoebe enters downstage right looking at her iPad.

Phoebe: *(talking to herself while looking at iPad)*: That Semitoned Pirates was appalling! One star definitely – title, title, title – where are those phrases – Oh – here we go: "Skimmed milk masquerading as cream." That should do it. *(Phone starts to ring/or vibrate)*: Yes, I've just reviewed the Semitoned Pirates. What's that? Can I review Idle Auntie? Well … I know nothing about the show, the genre, the company, the plot, the target audience … of course I can review it! It's just about to start! *(rushes into venue)*

Blackout: sounds of laughter and rapturous applause from Fred's show.

Phoebe comes out of venue looking at her iPad. Voice 1 and 2 enter to either side of stage.

Phoebe: Well that was easy enough! 5 stars for Idle Auntie and 1 star for The Semitoned Pirates ... Am I sure of all this? Yes – *(looks at audience)* I wrote it all down on my tablet. SEND! *(turn to back of stage)*.

Spotlights on Voices 1 and 2

Voice 1: These rooky reviewers! This one's sent an email entitled "Review for Idle Auntie and Review for The Semitoned Pirates". There are two attachments but she doesn't say which attachment is for which show.
Voice 2: How many stars are they?
Voice 1: One's got five and the other only one.
Voice 2: That Semitoned Pirates is by SoCoCoCo's son, Ralph.
Voice 1: Thought he was called Raiph.
Voice 2: Well whatever he's called he's bound to have had help, so he'll be the five star review – simples.
Voice 1: Glad we worked it out - It would be awful if we made a mistake and mixed them up.

Scene change: Short piano extract from: Things are seldom what they seem – H.M.S. Pinafore

Phoebe (Mabel) puts hoodie on and takes lanyard off.
Fred picks up a Three Weeks paper.
Voice 1(Ralph) puts waistcoat on and picks up a Three Weeks paper.
Voice 2 (Angelina) puts Lanyard on.

Scene 8: Reading the first set of reviews

SETTING: A QUIET ROAD NEAR THE FRINGE VENUE

Fred, Mabel, Ralph and Angelina are grouped in a madrigal type formation, Fred and Ralph are holding closed copies of Three Weeks.

Song 8 Melody: Brightly dawns our wedding day (The Mikado)
(last section of melody is omitted - end at the point the new lyrics end)

Fred, Mabel walk forward on the introduction while Ralph and Angelina remain slightly further back.

Fred: Well the first reviews are in.
All: Sure it's great, the shows fantastic.
Getting five stars would be magic
But we'll take it on the chin.
Yes we'll take it on the chin.

Fred opens paper.

Fred: Overplayed and overacted,
Mabel: Dialogue was too protracted
All: Whole experience below par.

One star... One star…
One star.

All: Don't despair, there's still tonight
Who knows we might get it right.
Fred: It's a failure it's a flop!
All: It's a failure it's a flop…
Fa la las
One star… one star… one star.

Ralph and Angelina walk forward, Fred and Mabel fall back.

Ralph: Hope my show is a success.
All: Please my parents, change career paths
Go to Uni, do applied maths
But I/(he)'ll take it on the chin.
Yes I (he)'ll take it on the chin.

Ralph opens paper.

Ralph: What a triumph, fringe high octane - *(scans review)*
Angelina: Lots of comments, all quite germane.
All: This young Company will go far…
Five stars...
Five/One star… Five/One star (split into singing "five" and "one" on last four notes).

Move forward/back into one line on last lines and strike pose to highlight it ends here – omit last section of melody.

Angelina: Oh Ralph. You must be so pleased – Five stars!
Ralph: Rather surprised if I'm honest - but my parents will be pleased. My biggest worry is the reviewer who's in tonight. They are notoriously harsh. I do so hope I get another good review so that I can make my parents proud. *(wistfully)*: Maybe then they will let me follow my dream.

Angelina and Ralph leave stage.

Fred: A disaster Mabel, that's what it is, a disaster. Nobody will come and see the show now.
Mabel: Don't worry Fred, there's another reviewer coming to the next show, they might give us 5 stars, you never know!

Fred: Mabel, I think we both know that won't happen, the reviewer hated it - and the reviewer ... the reviewer! You know the girl I told you about, who I met on the train?

Mabel: Phoebe? It can't be Phoebe, surely?

Fred: Yes, it's Phoebe. Well she wrote that review.

Mabel: But you were going to meet her at the Pooh Bar tonight.

Fred: Well, I'm not now. How could she be so cruel? But - as Idle Auntie's Director I need to pull myself together and *(melodramatically)* think of the cast. Mabel - tell everyone we're going to go to a show together tonight for a bit of team and morale building.

Scene change: Short piano extract from: Yes, 'tis Phoebe – The Yeomen of The Guard

Angelina (Ida) takes lanyard off, puts hoodie on and gets a stool.
Ralph (Rupert) takes waistcoat off, puts hoodie on.
Fred and Mabel move the trunk. Mabel puts flyers on the trunk. Each get a stool.
The three stools are placed round closed trunk (acting as table) with a variety of flyers on them, downstage right.

Scene 9: *Meeting John and taking the lozenge*

SETTING: AN OPEN AIR FRINGE BAR

Fred, Mabel, Ida are sitting round the trunk/table, looking despondent. Rupert is standing.

Rupert: I'll get a round in - 2 halves and 2 cokes? Do you think 40 quid will cover it? *(all nod as Rupert leaves)*

Rupert takes off hoodie and changes into a magician's cloak offstage (with flyers, wand, cards and lozenges in pocket).

Fred: OK team, what shall we go and see – comedy, dance, magic, theatre, circus?

Mabel: Well I don't care what we see so long as it isn't magic *(all groan in agreement)*. *(very seriously)*: It's not real magic you know, just illusions *(all nod)*. That's what really irritates me.

Fred: *(resignedly)*: OK Mabel, Anything but magic. What shall we go and see then?

Mabel: (picking up flyer): Here's one that looks interesting. An expose of alcoholism in the House of Lords … "The Peer and the Perry".

Ida: Or this. Set on the River Mersey … "The Ferryman and his Trade".

Mabel: There's so much choice!

John enters on the piano introduction, weighing up Mabel, Ida and Fred as three potential audience members.

Song 9 Melody: I've jibe and joke (The Yeomen of The Guard)

John: You want a show?
In half an hour?
Five star reviews,
Sold out last year.

Fred's team *(in turn):*
Well we could do,
We've nothing planned.
We're rather blue,
Our show's been panned.

Fred's team *(together):*
But not if it's a magic show
If that's the case then we'll forgo.

John: I know my trade is very much maligned.
Fred: You're just a genre that we can't abide.
John: How about I try and make you more inclined?
Fred: I really doubt that you can turn the tide.
John: If I perform some magic and it works,
Will you see my show and tweet and like my page?

John: Oh I can make you see it even though you think it irks,
A magic show performed upon the stage.
Oh I can make you see it even though you think it irks,
A magic show performed upon the stage.

John: All you do is take a lozenge, here.
Fred: Oh all right then, we'll join in, play pretend.
John: This is magic, so there's nothing you should fear.
Fred: I think a Fisherman has lost his Friend *(looking at lozenge skeptically)*.
John: Shows you hate you'll think you love, when it works
And those you love will send you in a rage.

All:
Oh these will make you/us love it, even though you/we think it irks,
A magic show performed upon the stage.

Oh these will make you/us love it, even though you/we think it irks,
A magic show performed upon the stage.

All start to leave – dialogue as leaving:

Fred: John – which venue's the show in?
John: Venue 70 – bottom of Cowgate, on Simmery Axe.

John exits.

Scene change: Short piano extract from: My name is John Wellington Wells –
The Sorcerer

Fred and Mabel move trunk out of the way to downstage left then take a stool each to back.
Ida takes flyers and stool to back.
All leave stage then Mabel, Ida and Fred re-enter after piano interlude ends.

Scene 10: After the magic show

SETTING: ON THE ROAD LEADING AWAY FROM VENUE 70

Mabel, Fred and Ida on stage.

Mabel: Un – be – lievable!
Ida: Why have we never liked magic before?
Fred: My best fringe show so far.
Ida; I'm going to tweet this – everyone needs to see this show.
Mabel: Wait a minute ...
Don't you realise what happened tonight?
Fred *(penny drops)*: ... Of course – we all hate magic usually.
Ida: The Magic Lozenges really WERE magic!
Mabel: So, because we hated the show we actually thought we loved it.
Ida: Amazing - they make you like what you hate and hate what you like!
Fred: *(as idea dawns on him)*: Wait a minute, wait a minute, don't you see? This
is our salvation!
Mabel: What?
Fred: If we get hold of one of those lozenges and give it to our next reviewer, then
when they see the show, which we now know the reviewers think is awful, the
lozenge will make them think the opposite and so they'll think it's great and give us
a good review!
All: Genius!

Fred: See you later – I'm off to Venue 70 to get a lozenge from John.
Mabel: Wait for me!

Scene change: Short piano extract from: Strange adventure – The Yeomen of The Guard

Fred and Mabel put trunk in position stage left (upended, at 90 degrees to front of stage, slightly open to act as box office) then go off stage. (Fred gets the Scottish £5 ready.
Ida (Angelina) takes hoodie off, puts lanyard on then stands behind box office.

Scene 11: Buying the lozenge

SETTING: OUTSIDE THE BOX OFFICE AT VENUE 70

Angelina is alone on stage, behind the box office, packing up as John enters.

Angelina: Good show, John?
John: Not bad.
Angelina: Good audience?
John: Biggest so far! Had four in tonight. Have you got much longer to work?
Angelina: No, finishing soon – just tidying up the box office then off to meet my friend, Jack.
John: Is he the street entertainer?
Angelina: Yes, but his partner Elsie has run off. She uses this app called "Strange Adventure" and has ended up getting married to a groom she'd never seen.
John: Never?
Angelina: Never.
John: *(pensively)*: Never seen.
Angelina: The Groom himself was to be wedded just next week at Gretna Green.
John: Gretna?
Angelina: Gretna.
John: *(pensively)*: Gretna Green
Angelina: Anyhow, when I finish I'm off to see if I can cheer Jack up, he's a bit down. His last text was very odd! See you tomorrow.

Angelina continues pottering about behind the box office, eavesdropping on the next conversation. Fred and Mabel enter.

Song 10 Melody: Kind Captain I've important information (H.M.S. Pinafore)
(Omit third verse melody)

Fred: Hey, John! That Magic Lozenge, can I buy one

To give the next reviewer in the bar?
Mabel: We want our show to fill its seats this Fringe Run,
we need a sure fire way to get five stars.

All: They/we need a sure fire way to
They/we need a sure fire way to
They/we really need a
sure fire way to get five stars.

John: Of course! I see my magic has convinced you
To be less skeptical of your bête noir.
(*Fred offers a Scottish £5*)
A Scottish note? Oh, OK I will make do.
This lozenge will ensure it gets five stars.

All: The lozenge will ensure it
The lozenge will ensure it
The magic lozenge
will ensure it gets five stars.

Fred and Mabel move upstage centre, looking at the lozenge.

Angelina: I can't help overhearing John, I'd like one
To help a friend impress his Ma and Pa.
If so, they may allow him theatre to shun.
He really needs his show to get 5 stars.

All: He really needs his show to
He really needs his show to
He really needs to help
His show to get five stars.

After the song Fred, and Mabel and Angelina head off stage, with Angelina leaving last.

John: (*shouting after Angelina*): Oh, Angelina – you do know how they work don't you? The reviewer will only think it's good if the show is really bad! They make you think the opposite! Oh, never mind, she's gone.

Scene change: Short piano extract from: See how the fates their gifts allot – The Mikado

Angelina gets a lozenge and a light up plastic glass.

38

Fred: Really? Oh, it's so encouraging to hear you, the great SoCoCoCo, say that. Did you have a show that did badly that you learnt a lot from?

SCCC: Err no, mine have always been fabulous successes but that's what other people have told me. I feel a strange bond with you, young man. You remind me a lot of myself at your age *(both strike pose again as piano plays: "The Nightingale sighed"/lighting effect).*

Melody: But tell me, who's the youth - then straight on (as in H.M.S. Pinafore) into the melody of: The Nightingale Sighed

Song 14 Melody: But tell me, who's the youth (H.M.S. Pinafore)

SoCoCoCo:
Excuse me:
What's that book, that I can see -
Its title is protruding on a string?

Fred pulls out the book which is attached by a string to his hoodie.

Fred:
Milne! First edition that was left with me:
A Foundling!

SoCoCoCo:
Pooh!
Pooh Bear!
Rejoice!
Rejoice!

Song 14a Melody: The Nightingale Sighed (H.M.S. Pinafore)

SoCoCoCo:
I placed you there
On the steps of the Savoy.
It wasn't fair
The Fringe was two weeks away.

Fred: It was two weeks away?
All: It was two weeks away.

Fred: I understand,

For our art we sacrifice.
I'll shake your hand,
Your good excuse will suffice.

SCCC: *(very surprised)*: My excuse will suffice?
All: Her excuse will suffice.

SCCC: I think you have inherited my talent
And I can see you really have some Mojo.
I'm going to make an offer rather gallant,
Will you take on the business SoCoCoCo?

Fred: I will take on the business SoCoCoCo.

All: He will take on the business SoCoCoCo.

Mabel and Ralph do a "screwing in the light bulbs" action on the last line, as if cheering.

Mabel discreetly exits with Ralph's maths book, changes from hoodie into lanyard and re-enters after Fred's "I skipped our date at Pooh Bar" line.

Song 14b Melody: A maiden fair to see (H.M.S. Pinafore)

Fred: I'm happy, yes it's true
But what am I to do
That Phoebe gave me one star.
My anger I've suppressed
But I was so depressed
I skipped our date at Pooh Bar.

All: He skipped his date at Pooh Bar.

Phoebe comes forward.

Phoebe: Oh Fred, I've just found out
Why did you have such doubt?
I though your show was super.
The office is a dive,
The one star show got five!
I made a novice blooper.

All: She made a novice blooper.

Ralph: Am I now off the hook?
I can't believe my luck
I'll go tell Angelina.
I'll leave the stage behind
As maths will stretch my mind
Forget this misdemeanor.

All: He'll leave the stage behind
As maths will stretch his mind
Forget this misdemeanor.

Scene 15: Returning to the flat

SETTING: WALKING ALONG THE ROYAL MILE

Fred: Why don't we all head back to my flat to celebrate?

Phoebe: Well, why don't we all head back to **my** flat to celebrate?

Fred and Phoebe walk hand in hand towards stage left, with Ralph and SoCoCoCo following.

Fred and Phoebe Together:
It's just over there *(pointing)*:
Waterloo House.
Door Numb'ring One.

Phoebe: What do you mean?
Fred: I'm renting.
Phoebe: But this is my flat!
Fred: Hang on a minute, when do you sleep here?
Phoebe: There's a weird curfew that we have to leave at 7.30am in the morning and come back at 8pm.
Fred: That explains it, we've been had. We leave the flat at 7.30pm and come back at 8am. Who could switch round a flat that quickly.
Phoebe and Fred: Gus and Mark?

SoCoCoCo and Ralph catch up.

SoCoCoCo: Did I hear somebody mention Gus and Mark? The fastest scene changers in the business? They did a show for me once and were the best I ever encountered - 3 settees … and an Aga. I've been trying to track them down for years to persuade them to join my company!

Re-position so that all four are in a straight line across front of stage, each reacting to the next set of lines.

Phoebe: So, let's get this straight: Fred has turned out to be SoCoCoCo's long lost son, abandoned on the steps of the Savoy at birth. Fred can now take over SoCoCoCo's theatre company, enabling her to retire. Ralph doesn't have to live up to his Fringe status any more, and can be reunited with Angelina, give up theatre and follow his dream of studying maths. Fred realises the Fringe office made a mistake - his show should have got five stars - and I am forgiven. John's delighted too, as now we all believe in magic! Meanwhile the flat situation has been discovered. Gus and Mark, the fastest scene changers in the business, will be reunited with SoCoCoCo and have a job offer with the company. Everybody's happy … although we've had some terrible news about Jack, the street entertainer … let's not dwell on that … But I can't help thinking that something is missing to make this scenario complete!

On "let's not dwell on that" the couples move to each side of stage, consoling each other, leaving space for Gilbert and Sullivan to enter.

Scene 16: Finale

SETTING: THE ROYAL MILE

Triangle "ding"/cast freeze.
Gilbert and Sullivan walk to centre of back of stage.

Gilbert: And that's as far as I've got – I'm stuck on this missing element! You see, I just can't do it without you, Arthur.
Sullivan: But Gilbert, it's obvious what's missing – I have just the melody!
Gilbert: (anxiously): Oh, hold on! It's not another one of your "Fa-la-las" is it?
Sullivan: *(exasperatedly)*: No, Gilbert, it doesn't have any "Fa-la-las" in it.

Triangle "ding" and cast resume.

Fred: Why don't we all sit down with a hot drink. *(dramatically)*: For what, I ask, is life, without a nice hot cup of tea in it?

Dramatic lighting – form ensemble on stage in typical "Hail poetry" formation.

Song 15 Melody: Hail poetry (The Pirates of Penzance)

All: Hail cup of tea, when freshly made!
Thou gildest e'en the Fringe's trade:
Hail, flowing caffeine se-di-ment,
All hail! All hail! Divine emollient.

Break out – pats on back/shake hands/high fives/congratulating each other.

Song 16 Melody: After much debate internal (Patience)

Each pair of the first eight lines are individually sung, then all sing together.

So they let the flat twice over,
How they switched it we're in awe.
Moving in and moving out
As we were going through the door.

Only one Fringe pair we know of
who could pull off such a switch.
if you need some quick scene changers
Gus and Mark are those you'd hitch.

All: If you need some quick scene changers
Gus and Mark are those you'd hitch.

So we've offered them the job,
Scene changers for SoCoCoCo.
It's all round a happy ending,
We hope you enjoyed the show.

It's all round a happy ending,
We hope you enjoyed the show.
It's all round a happy ending,
We hope you enjoyed the show.

During this, choreograph so that all (including Gilbert and Sullivan) end in a straight line for bows/thanks to technical team and pianist in time with the final phrases of the music.

THE END

Play out music: repeat last musical section of final piece.

Appendix A: Props list and distribution – as used in original performance

Stored between shows: Vintage Trunk, containing a score from every show
4 stools; 2 chairs (for G&S)
Piano/stool/stand/light/pedal

Back stage prop box: Mabel and Ida's hoodies
SoCoCoCo's Arty scarf and sunglasses
John's Magician's cloak, wand, cards, lozenges
2 mobiles (for fringe office scene)
2 light up plastic glasses

Ralph prop box: Beanie
Can
Hoodie
Lanyard
Waistcoat with name tag
Maths book
Buffet attendant's hat
Scotsman and Three Weeks

Fred prop box: Beanie
Can
Hoodie with book on string attached
2 Fringe programmes
Lanyard
Scotsman and Three Weeks
Flyers
Scottish £5 in pocket of hoodie

SoCoCoCo prop box: Angelina's Lanyard
Scotsman

Mabel prop box: Lanyard
3 notepads
Air stewardess hat
Mobile and iPad
Scotsman

Sullivan: Triangle, beater and string

Appendix B: Melodies and cues for Pianist

(In the original performance the scene change music was preceded by 4 beats where the cast stood frozen in position turned to the back of stage prior to the scene change lighting effect/music)

Song 1: *Then one of us will be a Queen*

Gilbert and Sullivan dialogue: **Cue: "Nothing new there then."**

Song 2: *Hark the Hour of Ten*

Scene change: *Little maid of Arcadee*

Gus and Mark sorting the flat dialogue: **Cue: "List and learn… List and learn!"**

Song 3: *Here upon we're both agreed*

Scene change: *I have a song to sing, O!*

Song 4: *Ring Forth ye Bells*

Fred's team preparing to go to the Fringe dialogue: **Cue: "Well, where we need to be in an hour is on the train to Edinburgh. Come on, let's go!**

Scene change: *A tenor all singers above*

Phoebe's team preparing to go to the Fringe dialogue: **Cue: "Let me explain."**

Song 5: *If you want a receipt for that popular mystery*

Phoebe group dialogue continued: **Cue: "Have a good flight and we'll see you up there."**

Scene change: *Comes the broken flower*

Ralph and Angelina meeting on the plane dialogue: **Cue: Passenger Angelina, come to gate and board: Angelina, Angelina, Angelina."**

Chorus of Bridesmaids short musical interlude as Angelina enters

Ralph and Angelina meeting on the plane dialogue continued: **Cue: "Well I don't see what difference that makes, Ralph."**

Song 6. *If you give me your attention*

Scene change: *Now to the banquet we press*

Fred and Phoebe meeting on the train dialogue: **Cue: "Oh - The Pooh Bar."**

Song 7. *None Shall Part us from each other*

Scene change: *Welcome to our hearts again, Iolanthe!*

Reading the first set of reviews dialogue: **Cue: "It would be awful if we made a mistake and mixed them up."**

Scene change: *Things are seldom what they seem*

Song 8: *Brightly dawns our wedding day*

Reading the first set of reviews dialogue: **Cue: "Mabel – tell everyone we're going to go to a show together tonight for a bit of team and morale building."**

Scene change: *Yes, 'tis Phoebe*

Meeting John and taking the lozenge dialogue: **Cue: "There's so much choice"**

Song 9: I've *jibe and joke*

Meeting John and taking the lozenge dialogue continued: **Cue: "Venue 70 – bottom of Cowgate, on Simmery Axe."**

Scene change: *My name is John Wellington Wells*

After the magic show dialogue: **Cue: "Wait for me!"**

Scene change: *Strange adventure*

Buying the lozenge dialogue: **Cue: I'm off to see if I can cheer Jack up, he's a bit down. His last text was very odd. See you tomorrow."**

Song 10: *Kind Captain I've important information*

John's dialogue continued: **Cue: Oh, never mind. She's gone."**

Scene change: *See how the fates their gifts allot*

Angelina giving Ralph the lozenge dialogue: **Cue: "Oh Ralph, if only you could leave the smell of greasepaint behind and run off to be an accountant."**

Scene change: *Behold the Lord High Executioner*

Song 11: *When the night wind howls*

Scene change: *So ends my dream*

Mabel: Cue: "SoCoCoCo is expected on the Royal Mile at any minute!"

Song 12. *Bridegroom and bride*

Song 13. *Spurn not the nobly born*

SoCoCoCo dialogue: **Cue: "You remind me a lot of myself at your age."**

Song 14 a, b and c: *But tell me, who's the youth…The Nightingale Sighed…A Maiden fair to see*

Fred: Cue: "For what, I ask, is life without a nice hot cup of tea in it?"

Song 15: *Hail Poetry*

Song 16: *After much debate internal*

(Note that there are a few occasions during the script where the piano plays a phrase from "The Nightingale Sighed")

Quiz for Gilbert and Sullivan enthusiasts

Those with a knowledge of G&S will have spotted that the script is peppered with G&S references. Here are a few, in the form of a quiz …

1. The characters in this show are named after G&S characters. However Fred, Gus and Mark have had their names abbreviated.
a) What are their full names?
b) What operettas do they feature in?

2. Gus and Mark come up with a creative flat letting scheme. Before collaborating with Gilbert, Sullivan wrote the music for a comic opera with this theme.
What is the name of the comic opera?

3. When Angelina is called to the plane, the phrase "Come to gate and board" mirrors "Come thou into court".
Who utters these lines in Trial by Jury?

4. Ralph is impressed by Angelina's right elbow.
a) What G&S character boasts that their right elbow "has a fascination that few can resist"?
b) In which operetta?

5. Ralph's middle name is Schwenck?
What famous lyricist also bears this middle name?

6. Phoebe asks the train attendant for egg or ham sandwiches, though he only has strawberry jam and some "fancy sounding buns".
a) What operetta features these foods in a rousing chorus number?
b) What are the buns called?

7. The train attendant taps his nose knowingly at the mention of sausage rolls. In which operetta is eating a sausage roll used as a secret sign?

8. The fictional A.A.Milne themed pub is called The Pooh Bar
a) What G&S operetta features a character with a similar sounding name?
b) How is it spelt?

9. Fred was found on the steps of the Savoy by a member of the pit orchestra – the Second Trombone.
Which G&S character adopted this as a disguise?

10. When sending the email with her review attached Phoebe comments: "Am I sure of all this? Yes – I wrote it all down on my tablet."
a) Which G&S operetta features the dialogue:
"Art thou sure of all this?"
"Aye, sir, for I wrote it all down on my tablets."
b) Which character states the last line?

11. When looking for a show to see Fred's team consider "The Peer and the Perry" and "The Ferryman and his Trade".
a) Which two G&S operettas have names similar to these as their alternative titles?
b) What are the correct versions?

12. Angelina and John have some dialogue referencing that "The Groom himself was to be wedded just next week at Gretna Green" "Gretna?" "Gretna." "Gretna Green."
a) This dialogue mirrors G&S lyrics from which operetta?
b) What is the Green called in the original version?

13. The street entertainers Jack and Elsie are referred to throughout the show.
a) In which operetta do these two characters feature?
b) Phoebe comments they have had "terrible news" about Jack at the end of the show. What might this be?

14. Fred suggests sitting down with a hot drink, using the words "For what, I ask, is life without a nice hot cup of tea in it?"
a) What is the similarly scanning Gilbertian line, which precedes one of the most beautiful of Sullivan's choral pieces?
b) In which operetta is this found?

15. The address of the flat is Waterloo House, Door numb'ring One.
a) In which G&S operetta does "a Waterloo House young man" feature?
b) What song title scans with Door numb'ring One?

16. On finding out who wrote his first review Fred and Mabel exchange the dialogue: Mabel: "Phoebe? It can't be Phoebe, surely?" Fred: "Yes, it's Phoebe."
16a) Which two G&S characters have a similar exchange?

16b) In which operetta?

17: Phoebe uses the phrase "Skimmed milk masquerading as cream" in her review.
17a) Which G&S character sings a similar line?
17b) In what way does it differ?

18: Ralph is continually interrupted on the plane when explaining who he is the son of. Which G&S character experiences similar interruptions, when trying to reveal somebody's parentage?

19. Ralph explains that his fate to become SoCoCoCo's theatre company's producer would be "Utopian" for real theatre lovers. What is the alternative title of the G&S operetta Utopia Limited?

20. A "dealer in magic and spells", also called John, features in a G&S operetta. What is his full name?

Quiz Answers

1a) Frederic, Marco and Giuseppe
1b) The Pirates of Penzance and The Gondoliers

2. Cox and Box

3. Usher

4a) Katisha
4b) The Mikado

5. W.S. Gilbert

6a) The Sorcerer
6b) Sally Lunn

7. The Grand Duke

8a) The Mikado
8b) Pooh-Bah

9. Nanki-Poo

10a) The Yeomen of The Guard
10b) Kate

11a) Iolanthe; The Yeomen of The Guard
11b) The Peer and the Peri; The Merryman and His Maid

12a) The Yeomen of The Guard
12b) Tower Green

13a) The Yeomen of The Guard
13b) Jack has collapsed, broken hearted (and may be dead)

14a) For what, we ask, is life without a touch of poetry in it?
14b) The Pirates of Penzance

15a) Patience
15b) Poor Wandering One

16a) Fairfax and Wilfred
16b) The Yeomen of The Guard

17a) Buttercup
17b) The milk is referred to as "skim milk"

18. Katisha

19. The Flowers of Progress

20. John Wellington Wells

06102020

Printed by Amazon Italia Logistica S.r.l.
Torrazza Piemonte (TO), Italy

17249459R00034